SPEED RACERS

RACING KARTS

Jane Katirgis and
Alison G. Norville

Enslow Publishing
101 W. 23rd Street
Suite 240
New York, NY 10011
USA
enslow.com

Published in 2018 by Enslow Publishing, LLC.
101 W. 23rd Street, Suite 240, New York, NY 10011

Library of Congress Cataloging-in-Publication Data

Names: Katirgis, Jane, author. | Norville, Alison G., author.
Title: Racing karts / Jane Katirgis and Alison G. Norville.
Description: New York : Enslow Publishing, [2018] | Series: Speed racers | Includes bibliographical references and index.
Identifiers: LCCN 2017021989| ISBN 9780766092747 (library bound) | ISBN 9780766094161 (paperback) | ISBN 9780766094178 (6 pack)
Subjects: LCSH: Karting—Juvenile literature.
Classification: LCC GV1029.5 .K37 2018 | DDC 796.7/6—dc23
LC record available at https://lccn.loc.gov/2017021989

Printed in the United States of America

To Our Readers: We have done our best to make sure all websites in this book were active and appropriate when we went to press. However, the author and the publisher have no control over and assume no liability for the material available on those websites or on any websites they may link to. Any comments or suggestions can be sent by email to customerservice@enslow.com.

Portions of this book originally appeared in the book *Kart Racers* by Alison G Norville.

Photo Credits: Cover, p. 1 Volodymyr Gatsura/Shutterstock.com; pp. 4, 7 chevu/Shutterstock.com; p. 5 ivanmiladinovic/Shutterstock.com; pp. 9, 13 Odelia Cohen/Shutterstock.com; p. 10 Rolls Press/Popperfoto/Getty Images; p. 12 imageBROKER/Alamy Stock Photo; pp. 15, 20 Christopher Perks/Alamy Stock Photo; p. 16 Carl De Souza/AFP/Getty Images; p. 18 Steve Mann/Shutterstock.com; pp. 22, 26, 29, 33 Image Source Plus/ Alamy Stock Photo; p. 23 Click and Photo/Shutterstock.com; p. 31 Alex Makarenko/Shutterstock.com; p. 35 A_Lesik/Shutterstock.com; pp. 37, 39 Jonathan Ferrey/Getty Images; p. 40 Anne Cusack/Los Angeles Times/Getty Images; p. 41 Tatiana Belova/Shutterstock.com.

Contents

1. Let's Race! 4
2. Karting History 9
3. Building Your Kart 15
4. Time to Ride 22
5. Staying Safe 29
6. Kart Racing 37

Glossary 43

Further Reading 45

Index 47

Let's Race!

1

Not many people can say they started racing at the age of eight, but Logan Sargeant can. The sixteen-year-old Florida native began kart racing in 2008. By 2017, motosport.com listed him as number one in a list of the top ten karting racers to keep an eye on in the future.

A Rising Star

Logan Sargeant may just be the next American racing star. After moving up from junior level racing in 2015, he won the season opener WSK Champions Cup in 2016. He races in the United

Kart racing is an exciting sport, and many car racing stars start their careers as young kart racers.

States and Europe. He wants to continue on a path toward Formula 1 racing and is now part of the Carlin Racing team.

"I am really looking forward to this coming season with Carlin. They have won the Championship two years in a row, so they are the obvious team to compete with in the British Formula 4 championship," Sargeant said. "It's going to be a very exciting year, and we are all going to be pushing to make it three titles in a row; I will do everything possible behind the wheel to make that happen."

Sargeant's family will be cheering him on; racing runs in the family. Logan's older brother, Dalton, is a full-time ARCA Racing Series driver who sometimes races NASCAR Truck Series.

What Does Racing Feel Like?

Imagine that you're a kart racer. Now is the big moment—the last lap of the Karting World Championship at Daytona International Speedway in Florida. You dive left into the infield on NASCAR turn 1. Your competition, number 19, is strong on the straightaways. You have to pass number 19 before you dart back onto the oval. You take the outside line. Then you swing hard to the left, with just a quick touch on the brake to set up the next right-hand turn. You barrel ahead, wide open, and leave number 19 in the dust.

Speed carries you up the bank of NASCAR turn 2. As you follow the track along the shore of Lake Lloyd, you hear 19 gaining on you. On the steep slope of NASCAR turn 3, he shoots in front! You duck into his draft as you take the final corner. When you catch sight of the flagman, you slingshot around. Side by side, you and 19 dash the final fifty feet (fifteen meters). You have him by a nose when the flagman waves the checker.

You won! Was it a dream?

An Elite Group

Winning a race at Daytona is unforgettable. You join an elite club. The club's legendary members include Richard Petty, Dale Earnhardt, and Kevin Harvick. How do these elite drivers handle the many turns? Daytona International Speedway's turns are banked 31 degrees. The steep bank lets drivers take the sharp corners without touching their brake pedals. This lets the racers go fast, but it also keeps karters safe.

A Quick Tip

Don't slide through a turn on your first lap of the day. Slick tires need to warm up before they can grip the track.

You can find a local track and race the course with other riders.

Get into the Action

You don't have to be a spectator watching kart races from the grandstands. You can drive—not just in your yard or at an amusement park but on a racetrack against other racers like you.

There are hundreds of kart tracks in the United States. You can probably find one within an hour of your home. Tracks hold organized races for drivers from the age of five and up.

Karting is a good way to start racing. It can be a family hobby, or it can be the first step in a professional driving career. There are karting groups for kids of almost any age, experience level, and budget.

About 45 percent of kart racers in the United States are under the age of eighteen. Karting is the ideal sport for kid racers! Karting is an inexpensive and fun way to join the world of motor sports.

The Big Leagues

The International Kart Federation (IKF) and the World Karting Association (WKA)—the major kart racing organizations—have about fifteen thousand racing members.

The IKF (earlier called the Go-Kart Club of America) started publishing rules for racing competitions in 1957. Their goal is to provide rules, enable fair and strong competition, and to make the sport as safe as possible.

The WKA formed in 1971. Today, it is the largest governing body for kart racing in North America. It holds five racing series every year: the Gold Cup series, Manufacturer's Cup series, Winter Cup series, Road Racing series, and Speedway Dirt/Speedway Pavement series.

2 Karting History

Art Ingels was a race car builder in California. In 1956, he designed and built the original go-kart. Other people saw his kart and created their own. Go Kart Manufacturing, the first business to sell go-karts, opened in 1958. Early mechanics borrowed gasoline engines from lawn mowers or tractors. The first company to make engines specifically for go-karts was called McCulloch. The company used its chain saw motor as a model for its special kart engine.

The first kart races were held in parking lots. Safety was a problem, though. Karts could spin out right in front of a group of spectators!

Karting history dates back to the 1950s. In this photo from 1970, a race official waves a checkered flag to signal the end of a race. The checkered flag is still used to mark the race's ending.

Tracks just for go-karts came later. Soon, drivers decided to make official rules for the new sport. They formed the International Kart Federation in 1957. The federation's rules helped make karting safe and fair.

Letting Go of the "Go"

Racers dropped the "go" from the name "go-kart" long ago. The sport is now called karting, and the vehicles are called karts. Today, "go-karts" are considered toys. Don't be fooled, though. Early go-karts were not toys. Serious drivers competed in these pioneering machines.

Karting Today

Gone are the days of building a kart in your garage. A lot of careful engineering goes into sleek, modern racing machines. Kart manufacturing is a billion-dollar business worldwide. Karts, engines, and tires are sent to the United States from all over the globe. A chassis (pronounced CHA-see) might come from North Carolina or Australia. Some engines come from Italy. Most tires are made in Japan.

You don't need to travel around the world to buy your kart, though. There might be a kart shop near you. You can check the internet for online stores. Most shops also have mail-order catalogs.

Today's racers have many track choices. There are three basic types of kart tracks—speedways, sprint tracks, and road race courses. Karting speedways are oval shaped. They may be paved or made of dirt. Sprint tracks are paved tracks with both left and right turns. Road race courses are the longest. Sports cars also use them.

Most NASCAR races are held on oval speedways, either dirt or paved. Formula One fans go for the winding curves of the sprint and road race courses.

A sprint track is paved, and drivers turn left and right along the course.

Put Yourself in the Driver's Seat

You've gone to a kart race. The action, sounds, and excitement have made you a motor sports fan. Now, how do you get started as a new racer?

Walk through the pits at a race. Talk to the drivers and their crews. Ask about the right racing classes for your age group. Find out if you and your family have the mechanical skills to work on a kart.

Then stop by the track office for other useful information. Sign up for the track's mailing list. Collect copies of the rule book and newsletter.

If possible, try sitting in a kart. Do you feel comfortable? You might even take a test drive. Many clubs have a "fun run" at the end of the day. They let rookies borrow a kart for a trial run. Give it a try, and see if karting is really for you.

Try out a kart by sitting in the driver's seat to see how it feels.

A Look to the Future

Twelve-year-old Isabella Robusto and her twin brother, Will, are avid kart racers. The siblings are from Fort Mill, South Carolina, and spend time with their father at the track.

"I've been racing for seven years," said Isabella. "I have run Bandoleros, and I have run some dirt sprint cars. We mostly do the big go-kart races. We race about eleven months out of the year in different things, but mostly karts."

Isabella was moved up to the Junior Class, while Will is racing in the Cadet Class.

"We like to race against each other to see who can do the best," she said.

And although she is only twelve, Isabella has set her sights on the future.

"I want to keep moving up and get to NASCAR," she said. "I want to keep moving up with faster cars and more competition."

3 Building Your Kart

Are you ready to buy your first kart? Search the internet for trade shows. At these events, people showcase new products at booths in a large building. Also look for swap meets, where karters sell used equipment at bargain prices. When you go, talk to the people who sell karting supplies. Many companies have brochures with excellent information. Trade shows and swap meets are great places to find a builder to work on your kart engine. In addition, experts often give classes at these events. They share tips on mechanics and driving.

At a trade show, watch carefully and never be afraid to ask questions. The presenters are glad to answer. They all remember their first time racing. Then, when you go home, read all the information you collected.

The chassis is the frame of the kart, which sits low to the ground. It needs to be strong so that all the wheels stay on the ground during turns.

Chassis

Your first purchase is the chassis, the kart's steel-tube frame. A sprint kart chassis is best for beginners. In this kind of kart, the racer drives sitting up. A sprinter can race on most tracks.

The other kind of chassis is called either enduro or lay-down. The driver lies on his or her back. This reduces wind resistance, so the kart goes faster. Enduro karts are used only in road races on long tracks.

An amazing amount of engineering goes into making a chassis. A kart has no springs or shock absorbers. The steel tubing must be flexible enough not to crack when speeding through the curves. It also must be stiff enough to keep all four wheels on the ground in the turns.

Tires

Next, you will need special tires. Karts that race on asphalt use flat tires called slicks—tires without treads. Their soft rubber grips the surface of the track without slowing you down. They are in complete contact with the road, giving you the best control.

Other tires have grooves in them for water, but most racers don't want to race on wet road conditions because it can be difficult to handle.

If you are going to take your kart off-road, you will want tires that will not slide when cornering or going over rough terrain. Get tires with knobs on them, because the more knobs, the more grip.

A note on tires: Once you start karting, make sure you always check your tires for damage. You may find cracks, cuts, punctures, or nails stuck in the wheels. Ask an expert whether the tire needs repair or replacement. If replacing, be sure it is the same type of tire. And it never hurts to keep a spare tire handy.

Slick tires are smooth—perfect for racing your kart on a track.

Body and Brakes

Some karts have fiberglass bodies. These bodies give the kart an aerodynamic shape. This makes it slip cleanly through the air.

Finally, you can't go fast without good brakes to help you stop. All karts use a disc brake on the rear axle. Karts in some racing classes need front brakes, too.

Engine

You've bought most of your kart parts—but you've got no power! Now it's time to choose an engine.

A four-cycle engine is a good choice for a beginning karter. Four-cycles are like lawn mower engines. They provide a top speed of 90 miles (145 kilometers) per hour.

An experienced racer might choose a two-cycle engine made for racing. Two-cycles allow karts to reach speeds of 130 mph (209 kmh). Some karts, known as Superkarts, can go 160 mph (257 kmh).

Next, you'll need an engine gauge, also called a tach-temp gauge. This instrument shows how well the engine is working. The gauge must have two readouts. The tachometer—tach for short—tells how many times the piston inside the engine is revolving each minute. This is called the revolutions per minute (rpm).

The gauge also must have a thermometer that shows the temperature, or temp, of the engine. A speedometer is also interesting to have, but it's not necessary.

To move the power from the engine to the wheels, you need a clutch. There are two kinds of clutches: axle and engine. Check the rules for your racing class, and then select the kind of clutch that is required.

The kart engine powers the vehicle.
You can see it here behind the driver's seat.

At the end of the racing season, many drivers sell used equipment as they upgrade for the next year. It's OK to buy used equipment. Look for clean, well-kept parts.

Finishing Touches

Before you're ready to race, you need a few more specialty karting items. Just like Indy cars, karts do not have built-in starters. You must have a starter to turn on the engine.

Different tracks require different gears to adjust your power. Ask around at your local track, and buy the correct gears.

Karts are very low to the ground. You will need a stand to raise the kart while you work on it.

Nearly every kart racing class requires a specific exhaust pipe. Check your track's rule book for the correct pipe.

Almost everything else you need at the track is in a common tool kit. Organize your tools so they are easy to find. Most drivers use a little wagon to carry their starter system and important tools around the pits. You don't want to waste time and energy looking for misplaced things.

Personalize It

No two karts look exactly the same. Lots of racers give their karts fancy paint jobs. Some look like tigers, while others are painted like dragons. One dentist painted a toothy grin on the front of his kart.

Another way to stand out is to name your team. Choose a name that sounds speedy, like Fast Cat Racing. Then have a print shop make decals for your kart.

Perhaps they could have the shape of a running cat. You could get T-shirts printed with the same design for your family and crew.

Stripes are a cheaper way to jazz up your kart. Auto parts stores sell easy-to-use stripe kits in many colors. Be creative!

Sometimes a simple design is best. But the only limit is your imagination.

Time to Ride

4

So, you are excited about driving a kart or competing in a race. What is the next step? Go to your local track to see if they have practice days. You can take advantage of this time to get used to your new equipment. When you walk around the pits at a race, stop and ask questions. Karters love their sport. They will talk about it for hours.

Practice the Basics

The first time you drive your kart, you might be surprised by its power. Be light on the throttle at first! Starting, stopping, and

When you first start driving a kart, get comfortable with the throttle, and practice your basic skills.

tuning your engine are other basic skills to practice. Learn to let other riders know that you are exiting the track, are slowing down, or that you have spun out and are still on the track by raising your hand in the air. If your engine quits while you are on the track, be sure to push your kart off the track right away, into a safe place.

When you first start riding, keep the setup of your kart (tire pressure, gears, etc.) the way the kart shop or driving expert had them. Once you are a more experienced driver, confident in your driving technique, you can start making adjustments.

Take advantage of all possible practice time. The more you practice, the better driver you will be and the more comfortable you will feel behind the wheel on race day.

Be a Winner

The joy of kart riding may be enough in itself. The fun feeling of racing on the track and engaging your mind and body in a fun sport is thrilling. But if you want to win a race, it takes hard work, not luck or tricks. Here are some tips that will help make you a true karting champ.

First, always arrive prepared on race day. Don't waste time at the track doing things that you could have done at home.

Learning the track is a major key to success. Be ready on the grid for each practice round. During track time you'll discover your line—the quickest path around the track.

You've probably seen how NASCAR drivers draft. That means they line up behind each other on the track during a race in order to go faster. Drafting works with karts, too. This is a valuable skill to practice. Make friends with other drivers in your class. Planning to draft will help all of you go faster.

Controlling your kart's slide in the corners is important, too. Once you've learned a turn, you will know when to brake. More time on the gas pedal—and less time on the brake—means greater speed.

Finally, be patient. Expect to make mistakes. What matters is what you do when you make a mistake. Turn each mistake into a lesson. It is important to keep exact records of your lap times—how long it takes to circle the track—both in practice and during a race. That is how you can tell if you're improving.

Driving School

Do you want to improve your karting skills? A driving school may be the answer. Driving schools are a good way to sharpen your skills. The teachers watch you drive, evaluate your strengths, and help you improve your weaknesses. A driving school is expensive, but it can be worth it.

The Atlanta Motorsports Park's kart racing school is one example of a driving school that puts you behind the wheel of a racing kart. Practice your craft on one of the world's most unique and challenging karting circuits. You will learn braking, starting, and driving in a safe setting.

Over the years, the Jim Hall Kart Racing School had more than forty thousand students. Some of them became famous as racers, actors, or musicians. Famous Jim Hall graduates include NASCAR drivers Brett Bodine and Michael Waltrip, former talk show host David Letterman, actor Kevin Spacey, and comedian Jerry Seinfeld. In the spring of 2017, Jim Hall started a new program, the Jim Hall Racing Club.

Racing Venues

NEW CASTLE MOTORSPORTS PARK

New Castle Motorsports Park in Indiana is the favorite sprint kart track of many racers. Former Indy car driver and Formula Atlantic champion Mark Dismore Sr., opened the track in 2004.

Dismore says, "This has been a labor of love. I planned to build the nicest track anywhere. It makes me feel good when people from all over the world tell me it is their favorite track."

Once you learn the curves of a track and have practiced on the course, get ready to win a race!

The New Castle track is used for kart races from 0.5 to 1.5 miles long (0.8 to 2.4 km). It has many thrilling turns and hills.

Cars also race at New Castle. Mini Coopers average 77 mph (124 kmh), and Corvettes average 89 mph (143 kmh). Believe it or not, karts are the fastest, at 93 mph (150 kmh)!

The New Castle track rents garage space to kart teams during races. Working from a garage is a luxury for any racer.

GEORGIA KARTING KOMPLEX

Georgia Karting Komplex is popular with dirt-kart racers from the southern United States. This track is a quarter of a mile long. It is flat, with low banking on the corners. Here, the fastest karts reach top speeds of 80 mph (129 kmh).

Great care goes into preparing a dirt track. A special clay is ground fine and then spread on the track. Machines pack the clay and roll it smooth. Before a race, the track is sprinkled with water to make the racing surface stronger.

Sprint karts race at the Georgia Karting Komplex nearly every weekend. As many as seven hundred entries fill the air with dust and let out the roar of Briggs & Stratton engines.

Dirt Racing

The sport of dirt-kart racing came from early stock car racing. Competition is just as fierce. Today, dirt racing is a training ground for NASCAR drivers.

ROAD AMERICA

Each year, hundreds of road racers from around the country go to Wisconsin to run at Road America. The track is more than 4 miles (6.4 km) long, with fourteen turns and steep hills. This course challenges even the best drivers to their limits.

Road America boasts that it is the fastest permanent road course in the world. Many kinds of vehicles race here. Top speeds on the front straightaway reach 200 mph (322 kmh). Average lap speeds are slower. Cars have average lap speeds of 135 mph (217 kmh). Motorcycles average 110 mph (177 kmh). Karts are not far behind, at 107 mph (172 kmh).

Road America is a world-famous racetrack. More than 350 motor sports events are held there each year.

The Kink, one of the most difficult turns at Road America, tests both the driving skills of the racer and the strength of the kart.

5 Staying Safe

As fun as racing karts can be, there is nothing fun about injuries. To stay safe in this sport, you need to wear the proper gear at all times. It is important to follow the rules and develop safe habits so that you spend more time enjoying kart racing and less time dealing with injuries or mechanical issues.

A professional driver's uniform is not just for advertising. It is vital safety equipment. Just like the pros, what you wear may make the difference between life and death.

Helmets

The most important piece of safety gear is your helmet. It protects your brain. Karts don't have windshields, so you need a helmet that covers your whole face. It must have the latest Snell approval rating. There are three classes of Snell-rated helmets:

1. **Snell SA helmets**. The SA stands for "Sports Application." These helmets are professional grade. They give the highest levels of impact resistance and fire protection in auto racing.
2. **Snell M helmets**. The M stands for "Motorcycle." These helmets are designed specifically for motorcycle racing and other motorsports. They give less protection than SA-rated helmets.
3. **Snell K helmets**. The K stands for "Karting." This is the helmet you will need if you start riding a kart. They meet the same impact standards of SA helmets but not the same level of fire-retardant protection.

How to Choose the Right Helmet

There are four features of a racing helmet design that you should get familiar with. They are the field of vision, lining, face shield, and ventilation. When you are shopping for a helmet, keep these features in mind.

Your helmet should fit you correctly. First-time buyers tend to buy a helmet that is too big for them. The helmet should feel as though pressure is continuously being applied around your cheeks and your head. Once you are properly wearing it, your helmet should not be able to be pulled off in any direction. If it moves quite a bit, that means the helmet is too big for your head. Just like a pair of shoes, your helmet will break in over time. So, buy a helmet that feels as tight as you can stand. Remember, to give you the protection you need, your helmet needs to fit just right.

Make sure your helmet, the most important safety gear, fits properly.

More Protection

Racers under the age of sixteen have to wear an SFI-approved chest protector. Young bodies have soft bones that bend. If you hit the steering wheel in a crash, your ribs could squeeze your heart. A chest protector will keep your heart safe.

Keep in mind that not all chest protectors being sold are SFI certified because they are used in other sports. So check that the chest protector you choose is properly certified.

Sprinters must wear a foam neck collar. This safety device helps protect the neck and collarbones.

A driving suit does more than look cool. It helps reduce road rash if your body drags against the track. Driving suits are made of strong fabric or leather, with padding on the elbows and knees.

To guard your hands, you have to wear gloves. Look for racing gloves with padding on the tops of the hands and grips on the palms.

New Is Better

Never buy a used helmet. A new one is always stronger. Look inside a helmet to find its Snell rating.

One Last Safety Check

When you are getting ready to race, you will make a final safety stop called a pre-race safety tech. A trained inspector will check five areas of your equipment:

1. **Brakes**—The inspector pushes the pedal to see how well the brakes work. No fluid may leak from the lines. There can be no cracks in the disc. He checks all nuts and bolts.

2. **Throttle**—After the pedal is pushed, it must spring back to the off position. He checks all nuts and bolts.

3. **Steering**—He turns the steering wheel to make sure the front wheels turn. He checks all nuts and bolts.

4. **Fuel system**—All the plastic fuel lines must be fastened tightly with safety wire or a wire tie. Nothing may leak.

5. **Helmet**—The inspector checks the helmet's Snell rating.

Gloves and a racing suit are more pieces of important safety equipment. Don't race without them!

If the inspector finds anything wrong with your kart, he sends you back to fix it. When you pass inspection, you get a sticker on your kart and on your helmet. This shows that you are ready to race. No kart is allowed on the track without a sticker proving that it passed safety tech.

Nuts and Bolts for Safety

Karts vibrate a lot. Even a tight nut can turn off its bolt. To prevent this from happening, drill a tiny hole into the nut and the bolt. After the nut is secured, slip safety wire or a cotter key through the hole. Then the nut cannot come off. Kart inspectors check the bolts for this safety feature.

Accidents Do Happen

You passed pre-tech, and you're wearing safety gear. You're safe, aren't you? Yes, but you can't prevent all accidents. Sometimes parts break, and unplanned events happen. Karting is a competitive sport. You need to do everything possible to prevent an accident.

Check your tires each time you go out. A worn tire may blow out and spin you into the path of another driver.

If you break down, move your kart off the racing surface. Wait for help in a safe spot away from the action.

Always keep an eye on the corner workers—the officials standing at the corners of the track. When an official waves a yellow flag, expect trouble ahead.

Never drive recklessly. Unsafe driving causes deadly accidents. Karts can't take bumping and pushing like NASCAR autos, because they don't have strong bodies. Treat other drivers the way you expect to be treated.

Finally, be confident. Most crashes can be avoided if you stay safe and follow the rules.

Colored flags key the riders and fans about what is going on during the race.

Flags

A green flag starts the race, and a black and white checkered flag ends it. What about the others? That is how track officials communicate with you.

Green—Beginning of the race; drivers are clear to speed up after a yellow flag

Blue—A faster racer is trying to pass; move over, and allow him or her to pass

Red—Slow down completely, and go back to the pits

White—Last lap of the race

Yellow—Slow down; trouble ahead

Black—Penalty; the driver who receives the wave must return to the pits

Black and white checkered—End of the race

6 Kart Racing

Be prepared! This is a motto fit not only for Boy Scouts but for kart racers as well. Preparation is the key to winning. Learn all you can before you go to your first race. Some kart clubs have special schools for beginners in the off-season. This is a chance to learn from experienced karters. The club may assign mentors to help rookies during their first season.

Equipment and Supplies

Make sure you have all these items before you head to the track:

- complete kart
- kart stand
- starter
- extra spark plugs
- tool kit
- gasoline tanks
- spray oil
- spray cleaners
- brake fluid
- hand cleaner
- flashlight
- fire extinguisher
- track rule book
- tire pressure gauge
- twisty wire ties
- nuts and bolts
- clutch oil
- safety wire
- stopwatch
- clipboard or notebook
- tape measure
- duct tape
- gears
- spare tires
- pit wagon
- paper towels

As you can see, the sport of karting involves a lot of equipment! How are you going to bring all of your supplies to the racetrack? You'll see lots of different ways. Some race teams pack up the family minivan. Others have the newest toy hauler—a combination of a motor home and a garage.

Decorate Your Bike

Bright colors and stripes make you stand out on the track. Your fans will see you easily in a pack. Decals make your kart look like a pro's. Most kart shops, racetracks, and businesses give away decals for free.

Motor Sports Little League

Just as professional baseball players often start out in Little League, many of today's professional race car drivers began in kart racing. Most Formula One racers, including the new star Lewis Hamilton, were karters. World champion Michael Schumacher loves karting. He owns kart tracks and schools in Europe.

Many NASCAR greats came from karts. Darrell Waltrip, Tony Stewart, and Lake Speed all ran kart races. In fact, Speed returned to his roots and joined WKA's fastest sprint class. Now he races a shifter kart.

Marco Andretti grew up in a long-time racing family. They started him in karts. In 1997, Andretti finished second at his first kart race in Flemington, New Jersey. In less than ten years, he was driving Indy cars.

Marco Andretti drives his kart in the "Stars of Tomorrow" karting series event at Road America in Elkhart Lake, Wisconsin.

Danica Patrick, today's most famous woman racer, began kart racing in 1992 at Sugar River Raceway near Brodhead, Wisconsin. Patrick went on to win several national karting championships. T. J. Patrick, Danica's father, says, "Danica just couldn't wait to start racing. I made it a rule that if she was going to do this, she had to learn something every time she went onto the track."

At California Raceway, an uncle gives his niece a hug before a kart race. Kart racing is a sport for the entire family to enjoy.

The Day of the Race

Many riders arrive to the race early or perhaps the day before if they had to travel a long distance to the racetrack. Although you will be anxious to hop into your kart and race, you'll have to take a few first steps before you're set to ride.

As soon as you get to the track, you will go to a sign-up booth. Here you will choose your race and pay your entry fee. There is usually a long line,

Racers line up before their race.

so try to arrive early. You might even be able to sign up online before race day.

Shortly after sign-up closes, there will be a driver briefing. Race officials will give you your race information and any special instructions you may need. This is a great time to ask questions. Don't be shy; other racers probably have the same questions that you have.

Officials will check your karts. Then it will be time to hit the track for practice. Pay close attention to how the track has changed since you last rode there. Be sure that you know how to enter and exit the track safely.

When it is race time, you will be shown your starting position. Races take place in qualifying heats that lead to the final race of the event. You will race with kids in your age group. Once the flagger waves the green flag, the race is on! Remember what you have practiced, and have fun.

Time for Family

Kart racing is more fun when the whole family is involved. Everyone can have a job on a family race team. One family member, the crew chief, takes care of the engine and other mechanical work. Other helpers are the record keeper, doctor, cook, and cheerleader. You are the assistant mechanic, as well as the driver.

A successful karting family works as a team. They all respect each other. At the end of the day, the whole crew feels good, knowing they all have done their best.

Glossary

aerodynamic Able to slide through the air easily.

axle The bar on which the rear wheels of a kart turn.

chassis A metal frame that supports the body and engine of a kart or car.

clutch A device for working the gears of an engine.

disc brake A type of brake that grabs a round metal disc to stop a vehicle.

draft A place behind a vehicle where there is lower wind resistance. Racers often ride in each other's drafts so they can go faster.

engineering The field of using science and math to design machines.

four-cycle engine A type of internal combustion engine used in karting and elsewhere. One stroke of every four is the power stroke. It is generally less powerful than a two-cycle engine, where the power stroke is every other stroke.

gears Discs covered with teeth that connect and transfer the energy from a vehicle's engine to its wheels.

grid The area where karts line up before going out on the track.

kink A sharp bend or curve.

mechanics People who work on engines and other parts of machines.

mentors People who guide or teach others.

piston A part of an engine that moves up and down within a tight sleeve in order to make the machine work.

pits The areas where race teams work on their karts.

racing classes Groups that race together because they have similar vehicles, engines, body weights, and ages.

rookies Beginners; people who are just starting to learn something.

rpm Revolutions per minute. Generally, the higher the rpm, the more energy the engine is producing.

SFI A company that sets safety standards for motor vehicles based upon scientific testing.

shock absorbers Parts of an automobile that make the ride feel smoother by absorbing, or taking up, bounces on a rough surface.

slicks Tires that do not have treads.

Snell approval rating A safety score that the Snell Memorial Foundation gives to helmets based upon scientific testing.

straightaways Long sections of a racetrack between the corners.

throttle The gas pedal of a vehicle.

treads The grooved outer surfaces of a tire that allow it to grip the road.

wind resistance The force of air against an object.

Further Reading

Books

Challen, Paul. *Kart Racing*. New York, NY: PowerKids Press, 2015.

Hamilton, John. *Go-Kart Racing*. Minneapolis, MN: ABDO Publishing Co., 2015.

Maurer, Tracy. *Go-Kart Racing*. Mankato, MN: Capstone Press, 2013.

Stevens, Eric. *Kart Competition*. North Mankato, MN: Capstone Stone Arch Books, 2013.

Worms, Penny. *Race Cars*. Mankato, MN: Smart Apple Media, 2016.

Websites

INTERNATIONAL KART FEDERATION

ikfkarting.com

Learn about the world's first kart racing organization.

WORLD KARTING ASSOCIATION

worldkarting.com

Visit this site to learn more about organized kart races, rules, and stars of the sport.

Index

A

Andretti, Marco, 39

B

Bodine, Brett, 25
brakes, 19
  safety check of, 32
British Formula 4 championship, 5

C

Carlin Racing team, 5
chassis, 17
chest protectors, 31

D

dirt-kart racing, 27–28
Dismore, Mark, 25
driving schools, 25
driving suits, 32

E

Earnhardt, Dale, 6
engines, 19–20
equipment and supplies, 38

F

flags, 36
Formula 1 racing, 5, 39
fuel system, safety check of, 32

G

gloves, 32
go-kart racing
  and family fun, 42
  how to get involved, 7–8, 12–13
  learning to drive, 22–25
  safety and, 29–34
go-karts
  building, 15–21

components of, 17-21
history of, 9-11
learning to drive, 22-25
modern, 11

H

Hamilton, Lewis, 39
Harvick, Kevin, 6
helmet, 30
safety check of, 32

I

Ingels, Art, 9

M

motosport.com, 4

N

neck collars, 32

P

Patrick, Danica, 39
Petty, Richard, 6
pre-race safety tech, 32-34

R

race day, 41-42
racing, what it is like, 6
Robusto, Isabella, 14
Robusto, Will, 14

S

Sargeant, Dalton, 5
Sargeant, Logan, 4-5
Schumacher, Michael, 39
Spacey, Kevin, 25
Speed, Lake, 39
speedways, 11
starter, 20
steering, safety check of, 32
Stewart, Tony, 39
Superkarts, 19
supplies and equipment, 38

T

tach-temp gauge, 19
throttle, safety check of, 32
tires, 17

W

Waltrip, Darrell, 39
Waltrip, Michael, 25
WSK Champions Cup, 4